SPINE SHIVERS

SPINE SHIVERS BOOKS ARE PUBLISHED BY STONE ARCH BOOKS
A CAPSTONE IMPRINT
1710 ROE CREST DRIVE
NORTH MANKATO, MINNESOTA 56003
WWW.CAPSTONEPUB.COM

LIBRARY OF CONGRESS CATALOGING-IN-PUBLICATION DATA

DARKE, J. A., AUTHOR.

ATTACK OF THE MUD CREATURES / BY J. A. DARKE ; TEXT BY BRANDON TERRELL ; COVER
ILLUSTRATION BY NELSON EVERGREEN.

PAGES CM. -- (SPINE SHIVERS)

SUMMARY: WHEN FIFTEEN-YEAR-OLD GREYSON BENNELL VOLUNTEERS TO HELP WITH THE
CLEANUP EFFORT AFTER A MASSIVE MUDSLIDE DEVASTATES HIS CALIFORNIA TOWN, HE IS
NOT EXPECTING ANYTHING BUT SOME HARD WORK — BUT THIS DISASTER WAS CAUSED BY A
VERY PECULIAR STORM AND HE SOON REALIZES THAT THE MUD ITSELF IS MAKING THE OTHER
VOLUNTEERS BEHAVE IN AN OMINOUS MANNER.

ISBN 978-1-4965-0220-9 (LIBRARY BINDING) -- ISBN 978-1-4965-0377-0 (PBK.) -- ISBN
978-1-4965-2356-3 (EBOOK PDF)

1. MUDSLIDES--JUVENILE FICTION. 2. VOLUNTEER WORKERS IN SEARCH AND RESCUE
OPERATIONS--JUVENILE FICTION. 3. HORROR TALES. 4. CALIFORNIA--JUVENILE FICTION. [1.
HORROR STORIES. 2. MUDSLIDES--FICTION. 3. MUD--FICTION. 4. RESCUE WORK--FICTION. 5.
CALIFORNIA--FICTION.] I. TERRELL, BRANDON, 1978- AUTHOR. II. EVERGREEN, NELSON, 1971-
ILLUSTRATOR. III. TITLE.

PZ7.1.D33AT 2016
813.6--DC23
[FIC]

2014046864

DESIGNER: HILARY WACHOLZ

PRINTED IN CHINA BY NORDICA.
0415/CA21500559
032015   008841NORDF15

ATTACK OF THE MUD CREATURES

BY J. A. DARKE

TEXT BY BRANDON TERRELL

ILLUSTRATED BY NELSON EVERGREEN

STONE ARCH BOOKS

a capstone imprint

TABLE OF CONTENTS

WOODSON

CHAPTER 1

The newscaster sat at the desk with a serious look on his face. Weather alerts scrolled across the bottom of the television screen. In Hollisworth, California, this had been a familiar sight upon turning on the local news station recently.

"We interrupt this broadcast to bring you an Action Ten News Special Report!" came the newscaster's urgent voice. "Good morning. I'm Robert Carlson for Action Ten News, bringing you more on last week's massive mudslide that wreaked havoc on the coastal town of Hollisworth, California.

It has been five days since a shelf of mud and debris broke loose and struck the quiet community, covering an estimated distance of two miles. The neighborhood of Winston Hills was hit most directly, destroying homes and forcing many residents to evacuate. For more on this story, we go live to Natalie Gates, who's in Hollisworth. Natalie?"

"Thank you, Robert," said the dark-haired woman dressed in a sleek black raincoat. She stood outside in the wind and rain as she gave her report. "The small town of Hollisworth is still reeling in the wake of the devastating mudslide that buried many homes and businesses just five days ago. This disaster occurred after a week of heavy downpour. That weather system has baffled many meteorologists, who cannot explain why it suddenly appeared or why it remained over Hollisworth for so long, not moving, before disappearing without a trace. It is the third time in just two months that this particular weather pattern has struck the United States. Just last month, sections of Washington, DC, were left underwater. And more recently, violent storms caused a similar mudslide in the Rocky Mountains outside of Denver.

"Thankfully, residents of Hollisworth were evacuated in time, and there have been no casualties to report. The Federal Emergency Management Agency, FEMA, has allowed some Winston Hills residents to return to their homes. Community support has been exceptional. Many volunteers are assisting on a daily basis.

"Right now, I'm standing in front of the Hollisworth Community Center, which has been buzzing with activity since the rainstorms struck last week. If you would like to be a part of the recovery effort in Hollisworth, FEMA has stations set up here at the center. It will be weeks, if not months, before the residents of Winston

Hills can resume their normal lives. Let's hope there's sunshine at the end of this terrible storm. I'm Natalie Gates, reporting live from Hollisworth. Robert, back to you."

"Thank you, Natalie. This has been an Action Ten News Special Report. We'll now return to our regularly scheduled programming."

CHAPTER 2

The screen switched from the news report back to the game show fifteen-year-old Greyson Bennell had been mindlessly watching while lying in bed, still in his pajamas. He checked the time on his nightstand clock. It was 9:30 in the morning.

Grey stood and stretched. An array of schoolbooks was scattered on the floor by his bed, piled atop one another. Because of the mudslide, Hollisworth High School — where Grey was stumbling his way through ninth grade — had been shut down for the remainder of the school year. The school hadn't been in the path of the mud. It was about a mile to the south of the disaster zone, just blocks from the community center where the news reporter had just broadcasted from, and about five blocks from the apartment complex where Grey and his mother lived. The high school's gymnasium was being used as a base for out-of-town volunteers, a place where they could eat and sleep. The locker rooms provided hot showers, and the cafeteria was serving fresh meals three times a day.

Grey stepped over the books, rummaged through his dirty laundry for the freshest-smelling shirt and shorts, and walked out of his bedroom. The apartment was quiet. His mother hadn't been home much lately. She was the Director of Community Services at the community center where the mudslide victims and volunteers were staying. So she pretty much lived there these days, and Grey had gotten used to cooking for himself.

He poked his head around the door to his mother's darkened bedroom. Sure enough, the bed was still neatly made.

She didn't even make it home last night, Grey thought.

At first, Grey had been proud that his mom was helping so many people. But now he was starting to worry about her.

A laundry basket filled with clean shirts and pants sat on the couch. Grey had used the washer and dryer down in the apartment building's basement all by himself for the first time the day before. Usually his mom did all the laundry. Thankfully, Grey hadn't shrunk anything or turned anything pink. He grabbed a fresh shirt and pair of shorts for his mother and placed them in a duffel bag along with a new toothbrush — still in the package — and a tube of toothpaste. Then he headed out of the apartment, locking the door behind him.

Even though it was barely ten in the morning, the late spring sun beat down from a cloudless blue sky. *Another hot day,* Grey thought.

It was also extremely bright. Grey was glad he'd snatched his red Angels baseball cap off the hook by the door before he left. He pulled it low over his eyes and hurried down the sidewalk.

The community center was straight down the road from where Grey and his mother lived. When he got there, it was swarming with people. Roadblocks had been set up around the parking lot. Cars, trucks, and vans snuck down side streets, their drivers searching for a place to park. Nearby, a section of street had been set aside for news vehicles. A couple of news vans had large antennae jutting from their roofs. Numerous reporters were milling about, microphones in hand, talking with one another and preparing for their newscasts.

Grey spied the dark-haired Natalie Gates from Action Ten News among them.

A Hollisworth Police Department patrol car was stationed at the entrance to the parking lot. A tall, muscular officer stood near it with his arms crossed.

Grey recognized him and waved. "Morning, Officer Kapoor!" he called.

The policeman smiled. "Greyson," he said. "How are you today?"

"Good, thanks," replied Grey.

Officer Kapoor was one of the four Hollisworth police officers who were often stationed at the community center entrance. Grey had gotten to know all of them, but Officer Kapoor was the nicest.

He pointed at Grey's cap. "Did you catch the Angels game last night?"

"Yeah, but I fell asleep during the eighth inning," Grey answered. "Did they win?"

"Yep," the officer said. "Scored the go-ahead run after the Yankees' pitcher threw a wild pitch. Catcher lost it in the dirt. It was crazy."

Grey whistled. "Cool."

"How's your mom holding up?" Officer Kapoor asked.

Grey shrugged. "Pretty good, I guess. But she didn't come home last night, so I'm guessing her tank is just about on empty by now." He held up the duffel bag. "Bringing her a change of clothes."

"You'll be a sight for sore eyes, I bet," Officer Kapoor said. "Head on in."

"Thanks," Grey said.

Officer Kapoor nodded as Grey slipped past the roadblock and into the parking lot.

Since the mudslide, the lot had been filled with delivery trucks bringing fresh bottled water, food, clothes, and bedding. Now that the recovery effort was underway, there was a line of short white school buses parked beside one another. As Grey approached the glass front doors of the community center, another bus pulled into the lot, its tires and sides splattered with mud.

Grey stopped and watched as the bus passed. It parked near the others. The doors swung open, and a group of weary-looking volunteers and residents stepped out. The volunteers each wore bright orange vests. Some of the homeowners carried full, black plastic garbage bags. One of them, a middle-aged man, trudged past Grey. He had a beard, and he walked with his shoulders slumped and his mouth tightly closed.

"How is it up there in Winston Hills?" Grey asked him.

The man turned. His eyes looked empty, hollow. Deep bags had settled under them.

The poor guy has probably been working nonstop, Grey thought.

"Fine," the man quietly croaked. "Everything is just fine."

Then he continued on his way.

Grey's face scrunched up in confusion. *Fine?* he thought. *How could anything about this whole situation be considered fine?*

Grey shook his head, casting one last look at the man before heading toward the community center's front doors.

The center was brimming with people. Grey felt like a salmon swimming upstream as he navigated the busy halls.

Approaching the cafeteria, Grey stopped. A line of white plastic tables had been set up. Volunteers were handing out brown bags of food and bottles of water. Grey figured his mom had barely had time to think — no way had she stopped for food.

Grey picked up a bag and a bottle. Then he made his way up to her second-floor office. He found her speaking with a volunteer, an older woman in a bright-orange T-shirt, and shuffling through a mound of papers on her desk. "Make sure there's room in the lot for a large semi-truck," Grey's mom directed. Her voice sounded tired. "We have another shipment of food arriving later tonight from the Red Cross."

"Got it," the woman said as she walked by Grey, who was leaning in the doorway.

"Thanks, Sherry," Grey's mom said, looking up from her paperwork. When she spotted Grey standing in the doorway, her face lit up. Grey walked over to his mom and gave her a huge hug.

"I brought you the finest meal in all the kingdom," Grey said, placing the bag on his mom's desk.

"I didn't know you could cook lobster," his mom joked.

He dropped the duffel bag onto a chair. "*And* the finest garments," he said.

"Well, aren't I just the luckiest mom? Thanks, kiddo." She cleared off some space on her desk. Then she added, "Hey, I saw Trevor about ten minutes ago."

"Oh, really?" Grey said. "Maybe I'll try to track him down."

Trevor Matheson was Grey's best friend. He and his parents lived right on the edge of the evacuation zone, but the mudslide had fortunately come to a stop less than a block from the Mathesons' front yard.

"Yeah," Mom said. "His parents are up in Winston Hills now, and there's a group of teenagers from different nearby schools heading up there shortly. I think Trevor's going with them."

"Weird," said Grey. Trevor wasn't normally the type to spend his free time volunteering. He'd rather disappear with his skateboard and find an abandoned lot to practice his kick flips and grinds.

Unless, of course, his parents are making him do it, Grey thought. *Or he's following a girl.*

Grey chuckled to himself as he remembered last summer when Trevor had joined the summer marching band at school, even though he hated organized school activities. All it had taken was one wink from the prettiest girl in their class, a flutist named Becky Driscoll, and Trevor was gung-ho about dressing up in wool uniforms and marching down streets in the swelteringly hot summer temperatures while playing the saxophone. He'd thought about quitting, but he knew this was his only chance to get Becky's attention. It hadn't even crossed his mind that Becky's boyfriend, a trumpet player named Nick, was also a member of the marching band. Typical Trevor.

Grey's mom sighed. Her blond hair was tied in a messy bun atop her head. She pulled it free, letting her hair topple down over her face and shoulders. Then she gathered it up again and tied it back in a ponytail. She peeled open the brown bag and took out the sandwich. "Thanks, sweetie," she said before taking the first bite.

"No problem," Grey said. "Gonna be another late night?"

"Afraid so."

"Where'd you sleep last night?" he asked.

She nodded toward her reclining desk chair and said, "Woke up with my head on the desk in a puddle of drool."

"Classy," Grey said, smiling.

"That's me," she said as she sniffed her shirt and wrinkled her nose. "Now where are those clothes?"

Grey tossed the duffel bag to her. "I'm going to try to find Trevor," he said. "Maybe I'll go up to Winston Hills with him. I've been meaning to help out after all. Is that okay?"

"Sure thing." The phone on his mom's desk began to chirp. "Be safe, sweetie," she said as she scooped up the phone and blew him a kiss.

"I always am," he said, heading out of the office. Grey walked back downstairs and out into the parking lot. He saw a couple of groups huddled together near the buses, including the group of teenagers. Sure enough, he spied Trevor among them. His shaggy brown hair was hard to miss.

The group's leader was speaking with them. She looked like she was a year or two older than Grey. She had olive skin and long black hair that reached down to the small of her back. Even from a distance, Grey could see that she was very pretty.

I was right, he thought, walking over to join the group. *Trevor's following a girl.*

CHAPTER 3

"'Sup, Trev?" Grey whispered in his friend's ear.

Startled, Trevor spun around. When he saw Grey, his shoulders dropped. "What are you doing here?" he asked under his breath.

"What do you mean, what am I doing here?" Grey asked. "My mom runs this place. Duh. I should be asking *you* what *you're* doing here."

"I'm volunteering," replied Trevor. "Doing my part."

"Funny," Grey said. "No really. Why?"

"I want to volunteer, Grey," he said. "Simple."

"It's the girl, isn't it?" asked Grey.

Trevor frowned. "Shut it."

"It's *totally* the girl. She's pretty. Who is she?"

"Don't you have better things to do, Grey?" Trevor muttered.

Grey squinted at his friend. "I'm getting the feeling you don't want me here," he said.

"Nice deduction, Sherlock."

"You didn't answer me. Who's the girl?" Grey asked. "What's her name?"

"Can I help you guys with something?" The voice stopped Grey in his tracks. His heart skipped a beat. He turned to face the front of the group.

The group leader was staring at Trevor and him. She had striking green eyes, the kind that made Grey's knees turn to putty.

The rest of the group, many of them around the same age as he and Trevor, also had their eyes on him.

Grey rubbed the back of his neck with one hand and shook his head. "I-I'm good," he stammered. "No help needed."

"Okay," she said. "Well, if you're part of this group, please listen up."

"Yeah. Of course. Listening up," Grey replied. He saw Trevor roll his eyes. Grey elbowed him in the stomach.

The girl turned back to the group. "You will each be assigned a group, and you will be given bags and gloves to help. Don't do anything you think might be dangerous, and if you feel uncomfortable at any time, please stop and find me."

She handed out orange vests identical to the ones Grey had seen the other volunteers wearing. When she handed him a vest, he meekly said, "Thanks." He could hardly look at her. Trevor was even worse. He could barely mutter the word.

Grey slid the vest on over his T-shirt and waited while the group of volunteers began to board the bus. Just then, he realized he should let his mom know he'd decided to go. He quickly pulled his phone out of his pocket and sent her a brief text: *Volunteering w/ Trevor.* Then he pocketed the phone again.

He and Trevor found a seat in the middle of the bus. Grey sat closest to the window.

"Hey!" A girl Grey's age popped up from the seat behind them. Her blond hair was pulled into pigtails, and she wore a visor and sunglasses. She leaned over and rested her chin on the green plastic seat.

"Uh, hi," Grey said.

"Do you guys live here in town?" she asked. "Or are you just here helping out?"

"We live here," Grey answered.

"So you go to Hollisworth High School?" the pigtailed girl asked.

Grey nodded. "Yeah."

"Got it," she said, nodding back. "We're staying there tonight while we're in town. My family, that is. My twin brother is here, too, but he's at the back of the bus. His name is Andy. I'm Summer. Summer Young."

"I'm Greyson. That's Trevor," he said, pointing a thumb toward his friend.

"Hey," Trevor said, though it was clear that his attention was directed toward the front of the bus, where the beautiful group leader stood speaking to the bus driver.

"Did either of your houses get hit by the mudslide?" Summer asked. She drummed the top of the seat with both hands.

Grey shook his head. "My mom runs the community center, though."

"Whoa," she said. "That's gotta be nuts."

"Yeah, it is," said Grey.

"We live near Redding," Summer said. "Usually just an hour drive, but because of the flooding, it took us about three to get here this morning."

The bus rumbled to life, jolted forward, and they began their trip to Winston Hills. As the bus pulled out of the parking lot, Summer slid back down and out of sight.

Grey sat back and gazed out the window. It was amazing. In this part of Hollisworth, it looked like nothing had happened. Sure, there had been rain. Enough to overwhelm the drainpipes and flood ditches and temporarily turn the Burger King parking lot over on Kaufman Street into a lake. But Winston Hills and its surrounding neighborhoods — the ones struck by the mudslide — were higher in the foothills, where you could see all the way out to the Pacific Ocean.

The bus slowly made its way through town, passing the pizza joint Grey and Trevor often hung out at. It was within walking distance of Trevor's house and had a ton of arcade games. Then, continuing uphill, they passed the road to Trevor's house. The bus rattled and roared as it climbed.

The farther they went, the more destruction Grey saw. First, one fallen tree. Then a whole thicket of trees toppled over like dominos. Their roots had torn free of the ground and were stretching up to the sky. Clumps of grass and mud clung to them. Where there had once been lawns, there were now layers of debris, sediment, sand, twigs, leaves, rocks, and clay.

They reached a checkpoint at the edge of the evacuation zone and came to a stop. A construction vehicle with an enormous mud-coated plow on its front drove by in the other direction.

It must be clearing the roads, Grey thought.

Grey also spotted a white truck with the FEMA logo on the side. A woman in a blue jumpsuit, a hardhat, and heavy-duty boots stomped toward the bus, a walkie-talkie in one hand. She spoke into it as she pointed forward, and the bus began to move again.

The bus moved slower now, and the damage they were passing was far more severe. Entire houses had been felled by the mud and rain, leaving nothing but splintered skeletons of wood and stone. Others remained standing but leaned to one side, threatening to fall over. Fallen trees and shrubs lay everywhere. In some places, where relief workers had already been clearing the damage, the sides of the roads were strewn with stacked wooden planks and logs and piles of debris. There was no grass, only mud. Grey couldn't see where one lawn ended and the next began.

Finally, the bus turned onto a cul-de-sac at the edge of the damaged area. Grey saw a handful of people wandering over the hills of mud, most of whom weren't wearing the bright-orange volunteer vests.

They must be homeowners, he thought. *Well . . .* former *homeowners.*

Grey's heart broke when he saw them scouring through the wreckage. They looked lost and tired. He imagined himself as one of them, searching for bits and pieces that might remain of his former life.

With a hiss of its brakes, the bus came to a stop. The driver pulled a lever, and the doors creaked open. The beautiful girl at the front of the bus stood. "All right, everyone," she said. "This is the checkpoint. Please gather at the front of the bus."

The busload of teenagers stretched in their seats. Many continued to stare out the windows, amazed at what they saw. Then, one by one, they filed off the bus and into the muggy, late-morning heat.

CHAPTER 4

The bugs were far worse than Grey had expected. As he stepped off the bus, he immediately swatted a large mosquito from his sweaty neck. And the air. It was so thick that Grey's breath seemed to catch in his throat. It smelled damp, like clay and earthworms and rain. He wiped his forehead with one bare arm, silently wishing he had a towel or bandana with him.

Summer stood beside him. She was shorter than Grey by a foot. She wore a backpack over her vest. "Bug spray?" she asked, holding out an aerosol can.

"Thanks," Grey said. He took the can, stepped away from the growing crowd, and sprayed his arms and legs. Then he sprayed a cloud of it in front of him and walked through it, making sure to hold his breath and keep his eyes shut.

"I have sunscreen, too," Summer said.

"Gimme." Trevor snatched the can from Grey. He disappeared into a haze of bug spray and then tossed the can back to Summer. "Wow," he said. "Whoever owns *that* place is awfully lucky."

Grey followed Trevor's gaze to the south side of the cul-de-sac, beyond the bus. A lone house stood tall in the middle of the damage. Its white siding was heavily speckled with mud, and a small grove of trees in the yard had toppled over in the mudslide and were now stacked like firewood beside the home.

"How is that house standing?" Grey asked.

"Andy and I have been to a few different disaster sites, and there always seems to be one building that survives," Summer said. "Like someone or something is looking out for it."

"Creepy," Trevor said, shaking his head. But he was still looking over at the beautiful team leader, who was standing by the door to the bus.

Beside her was a man in his thirties. He was deeply tanned, with more muscles than Grey thought could possibly exist except on one of those old sculptures of Greek gods or something. He wore wraparound sunglasses and a hardhat.

The man raised his arm to get everyone's attention. "Listen up, volunteers!" he said in a commanding voice. "My name is Finn. If any of you need anything while on-site, please don't hesitate to communicate with either myself or Mira." He nodded at the beautiful girl.

Mira, Grey thought.

"Mira," Trevor whispered. "I'm going to marry her."

Grey rolled his eyes.

"We will now be splitting up into teams of four," Finn continued. "Please seek out and assist any homeowner you can. Avoid dangerous structures, and remember to be safe. That is all."

The two boys waited while Mira began the process of separating the group of teenagers. When she reached Grey and Trevor, she said, "You two —"

"They're with us!" Summer piped up. She stood next to a boy now. He was tall, with long, lean features, shoulders that slumped forward a bit, and the same blond hair as Summer.

Must be her twin brother she mentioned, Grey thought.

"We are?" Trevor asked, confused.

"Oh. Okay then," Mira said as she moved on to the next two volunteers.

Summer waved for Grey and Trevor to join her and Andy. "This is my brother," she said.

"Hey." Grey nodded at him, and Andy waved.

Grey looked over at Trevor. His friend looked upset. "What's wrong with you?" he asked.

Trevor sighed and waved a hand in Mira's direction. Then he said, "I was hoping, you know, to help our fearless leader. Get to know her."

"Oh, come on," Grey said. He grabbed Trevor's arm and began to drag his friend away from the checkpoint and toward the homes.

"Goodbye, sweet Mira," Trevor said dramatically, but quietly enough that Mira wouldn't actually hear him. "I love you . . ."

The foursome began to walk down the block, into the mud-caked disaster area. They had to tread carefully. Trevor stepped on a soaked teddy bear that was holding a pink heart with the words "I WUV YOU" on it, and Grey nearly trampled a painting of a ship navigating rough waters with a broken wooden frame.

Nearby, a woman crouched in what must have been her front yard. The house behind her was mostly still standing. Its front door and windows were missing, but otherwise it looked unharmed. The garage next to it had not fared as well, though. It had fallen over and was half-buried in mud and rocks.

The woman was in her fifties, with wispy brown hair hidden under a straw hat. Her sweater, once yellow, and jeans were covered with mud.

As the four teens approached, the woman stood and sniffled. She wiped her tears away with one dirty hand.

The woman turned to face them. "Oh. Hello," she said. Her eyes were very red, and Grey could tell that she had been crying.

She's probably been crying for days now, he thought.

"Hi," said Summer. "Can we help you with anything?"

The woman removed her hat. Her shoulders sagged with relief. "That would be lovely," she said.

Summer, who had taken the lead in their group, introduced the other three.

"My name is Mary," the woman said. "Mary Pressman. My husband and I live — well, *used to* live — here."

"Where is your husband?" Andy asked. It was the first time Grey had heard him speak.

"He died last year," Mary said quietly. "It's just me now."

Summer removed the plastic bag from her pocket and said, "Let's gather your belongings, Mary."

Mary led them toward the broken house, pointing to one of the shattered windows. "That was the living room," she said. "I've only peeked in there. I don't know if there's anything worth saving, but I'd like to check."

Grey finally spoke up. "Is there anything in particular you're hoping to find?"

Mary sighed. "Most of my stuff is just that — *stuff*. But isn't that always the case? You don't really realize what's important until you lose it all." She paused for a moment. "There were a few photo albums, though. Family pictures. My heart would absolutely soar if I found out they're all right."

Mary walked over to the broken front door of her house, the same door she'd probably walked through for many, many years. She pushed it open and disappeared inside.

CHAPTER 5

Summer and Andy stayed in the front yard, waiting for Mary to reappear, while Grey and Trevor began to explore the rest of the property. Around back, near what used to be Mary's deck, Grey found a ceramic teakettle stuck in the mud. Treating the teakettle as if it was the skull of a dinosaur, he used his fingers to dig around the edges until he could pull it from the earth. It was amazingly intact. He placed it in his bag and continued on his way.

Trevor found a few framed photos, their glass broken and, in some cases, the photos themselves scratched by glass shards. In one, Grey saw a smiling Mary standing on the deck of a boat with her hair swept back and a large smile on her face. Another was a photo of Mary and a large, muscular man with a silver beard and glasses.

That must be her husband, Grey thought as Trevor bagged the photos. *Mary will be glad we found that.*

As Grey and Trevor walked around the house, a quiet rumble began to shake the ground near them. It was followed by a wet sucking sound.

"What was that?" Trevor asked.

Grey took a step away from the house. "I have no idea," he said. "An earthquake?"

"Oh, that'd be just about perfect," Trevor muttered.

The sound stopped suddenly.

Grey walked around the side of the house. He saw Summer and Andy in the yard. They were crouched down, picking items out of the dirt.

"Did you guys feel that?" Grey asked.

Summer looked confused. She craned her head around. "Feel what?"

Grey opened his mouth to respond but then stopped. He wasn't sure how to explain it. And if Summer and Andy hadn't felt it, then it must not have been as threatening as he'd thought.

"Never mind," Grey said. He waved one hand before adding, "Is Mary still inside the house?"

"Yeah," said Summer. "She hasn't come out yet."

"We should make sure she's okay," Grey said. He began to walk around the house toward the front entrance.

"Grey!" Trevor suddenly called from the backyard. "Dude! Check it out."

Grey stopped and hurried back to where Trevor stood. His friend was near the garage — or what remained of it — looking down at his feet. There in the mud was the corner of a mostly buried item.

Trevor knelt down and examined the corner. "I think it might be a photo album," he said.

Together, Grey and Trevor dug out the item with their bare hands. Where it wasn't smudged with dirt and grit, the item was jet black. As they finally pried it loose from the hard-packed earth, Grey saw that it was, as Trevor had said, a photo album.

Just what Mary was hoping to find! he thought.

It was like striking gold. Grey pried the album open, checking to see if the pages were still undamaged. The white page edges were warped by water, and in a few places, the plastic covering was wrinkled or torn.

Surprisingly, though, the photos taped inside were still there, undamaged.

Grey carefully turned the pages as he looked through the album. It seemed like Mary had made the album a sort of scrapbook. A number of pages included stamps or cut-out letters or plastic decorations. One page included a small plastic palm tree and a postcard from the Bahamas. A photo of Mary and her husband, both wearing bright floral shirts and holding colorful drinks, was glued beneath the postcard. It looked like it had been taken on the same boat as the framed photo Trevor had found earlier.

Grey closed the album and wiped the mud off the cover. Then he placed it in his plastic bag along with Mary's other possessions.

He peered back into the small hole that he and Trevor had dug. It was not terribly deep, maybe a foot or so. There was another item hidden underground, a thin box of some sort. It was cardboard, for sure.

Grey reached down for it. As he did, the small piles of dirt and rocks at the edge of the hole caved in, swallowing his hand and wrist.

"Ah!" he shouted in surprise. His fingers wrapped around the side of the thin box, and he tried to pull his hand free from the dirt. But it wouldn't budge.

It was almost like the dirt around his wrist and hand was holding on to him.

"What is it?" Trevor asked.

"My hand . . . is stuck," Grey said. He grunted and pulled. "How is it . . . stuck?" Grey was starting to panic, but never for a second did he think about giving up his hold on the box.

Trevor grabbed his arm near the elbow and helped pull. Grey twisted his wrist, clamping his fingers down on the box. Finally, he was able to free both his hand and the item he was holding.

"Bizarre," Grey said, looking down at the hole.

He shook his head, baffled. Then he opened the box. Inside was a beautiful white photo album, trimmed in gold flecks and untouched by the mud. It crackled as Grey opened it. On the very first page was an old color photo, taken many years ago. It filled the page. In it, a much younger Mary stood at a church altar in a wedding dress. Her new husband, wearing a pale blue suit and bow tie, stood beside her.

"It's their wedding photos!" Grey exclaimed. "Jackpot!"

He closed the album, slid it back into the box, and stood. "Mary!" he shouted. He tucked the box under his arm and began to jog back toward the house as quickly as he could over all the wreckage.

Summer and Andy were still searching the front yard. They stood up and looked at

Grey as he rounded the house. "Is Mary still inside?" he asked.

Summer nodded.

"Mary?" Grey called. He stepped over a pile of cracked siding from the front of the house. He reached the cement front steps just as Mary appeared in the open doorway. She looked much more tired now than she had when she'd entered the house. Her eyes looked empty, lost.

She could use good news, Grey thought.

He held up the box containing the wedding album and said proudly, "Look what Trevor and I found."

He expected Mary to cry. To hug them. To shower them with praises and leap up and down in excitement and hold the box to her chest and promise to never let it out of her sight for the rest of her life.

Instead, Mary said in a raspy, gravelly voice, "Place it in the bag with all the rest."

Wait, what? Grey thought.

Earlier, she had said that the only thing she hoped to recover in this tragic mess was her photo albums. How overjoyed she'd be if she found out the albums had survived the mudslide.

And they *had*.

So why is she acting like she no longer cares? he wondered. *And what's with her voice? And her eyes? She looks sick all of a sudden.*

"Is everything all right?" Grey asked her. "Are you feeling okay?"

"Fine," Mary said, staring at him with her hollow eyes. "Everything is just fine."

Grey chewed on his bottom lip and watched as Mary proceeded to step out of the house and back into daylight. She appeared tired now, her shoulders slumped. She didn't seem to care that Grey and his friends were helping her.

Grey did as she requested, sliding the box into the plastic bag. Then he tied the bag again and hoisted it over one shoulder.

With one last suspicious look at Mary — who was now wearily rummaging through a stack of trash — Grey joined Trevor, Summer, and Andy as they continued to pick through the rubble for hidden treasures.

CHAPTER 6

An hour later, the volunteers broke for lunch. A van from the Red Cross was parked alongside the bus Grey and the others had ridden up in. The van's back doors were open wide. Two volunteers stood there, handing out food from large blue coolers. A small line had formed. Grey and the others joined it.

He looked around for Mary and spotted her waiting to board a bus. This one had come to pick up any volunteers or residents who were either too tired to continue or just needed a break. At Mary's feet were the black plastic bags Grey and his friends had filled with her belongings. *She doesn't seem to care much about them,* Grey thought as he watched her begin to drag the bags across the jagged, dirty pavement like they were filled with trash.

In fact, everyone who stood in line for the second bus seemed just like Mary — tired and emotionless.

It's been a very long week, Grey thought. *I can't even imagine what's going through their heads right now.*

"Sandwich?" Grey had reached the front of the line. One of the Red Cross members, a young woman, held a sandwich wrapped in cellophane and a paper towel out for him. She smiled politely.

"Thanks," Grey said as he took the sandwich. The other volunteer, a man in his twenties, handed him a bottle of water and an apple.

Grey found a spot to sit on the curb, away from the main group, and Trevor joined him. Soon enough, Summer and Andy were also settling down beside them on a dry patch of cement with sandwiches of their own.

Grey downed half of his water in three long swallows. It was ice cold, and it tingled as it slid down his parched throat. He took off his baseball cap, which was now coated in sweat, and placed it on one of his knees. Then he rolled the bottle along his forehead, smearing the sweat and dirt across his face with the bottle's condensation. He used the paper towel to wipe his face clean.

Mira walked past them. She cupped her hands around her mouth and said to the mass of people, "Anyone who's heading back to the community center, your bus leaves in fifteen minutes. If you're staying with me for the afternoon, enjoy your lunch and we'll set out again shortly."

Grey looked at Trevor and said, "I feel like I already know the answer, but —"

"Oh, we're staying," Trevor interrupted. Then he dramatically bit into his sandwich, never taking his eyes off Mira. She sat down nearby on a fallen tree trunk next to Finn, who laughed and took a large bite of his sandwich.

He took down half of that in a single bite, Grey thought. But while Finn was jovial, Mira sat calmly, saying nothing and eating nothing.

Grey didn't mind sticking around for the afternoon. He had spent the past five days watching the news and seeing his mother working tirelessly day and night. And really, it all had been making Grey feel pretty worthless. But being up in Winston Hills, where he could lend a hand instead of sitting on the sidelines as a spectator, changed all of that.

Grey took a bite of his sandwich. The bread was a little soggy, and they'd certainly rationed the ham and cheese, but after all his hard work that morning, it tasted like the best sandwich he'd ever eaten. His grumbling stomach thanked him for it, and he polished it off in no time.

"Hey," Summer said, shielding her eyes with one hand while pointing with the other off to her left, "is somebody still up in that house?"

Grey followed her finger, cramming his baseball cap back on his head to block out the glare of the sun. She was pointing behind the buses at the lone house that still stood mostly undamaged.

"I don't see anything," Trevor said, his mouth full and his words muffled.

"Upstairs," Summer said. "In the window on the left. It looks like there's a silhouette of a person up there."

Grey squinted up at the window and, sure enough, it *did* look like there was somebody inside the house.

"It's probably just shadows," Andy said.

Grey studied the silhouette, waiting to see if it moved away from the window.

"It's probably the dude who owns the place, working instead of breaking to eat like the rest of us," Trevor suggested.

"Yeah," Summer replied, turning her attention back to her lunch, "you're probably right."

"I usually am," said Trevor. He smiled and then crammed the last bite of his sandwich into his mouth.

When they'd finished their lunch and had thrown their garbage into a plastic barrel near the Red Cross van, Trevor said to Grey, "Okay, I'm gonna do it."

"Do what?" Grey asked.

"I'm going to talk to her." Trevor exhaled loudly and shook his hands at his sides as if to pump himself up. "I'm totally going to talk to Mira."

"Oh, man," Grey said. "I can't wait to watch *that* train wreck."

"Knock it off," Trevor snapped. "You're not helping."

"Sorry," said Grey.

Trevor sighed. "Do you have a breath mint?"

"I'm volunteering to clean up after a natural disaster. Why would I have breath mints?" Grey replied.

"Good point. Wish me luck."

"I'll wait for you," Grey said.

Then he watched as Trevor strode toward the bus, where Mira was now speaking with one of the drivers. As Trevor passed the Red Cross van, it honked its horn and drove off down the road, back toward the safety zone. Once it left, Grey let his eyes drift back up to the house where he'd seen the silhouette in the window.

It was no longer there.

"Huh," Grey said to himself.

A number of volunteers and homeowners had opted to go back into Hollisworth, leaving only a handful of people — no more than two dozen, by Grey's estimate — to help for the afternoon. Summer and Andy were among the teenagers who'd stayed. Summer was perched on the trunk of a fallen tree, scoping out the nearby yards to see where they should continue their cleanup efforts. Andy was speaking with a man in his sixties whose balding head gleamed bright red in the sunlight. The man was pointing at the cracked structural remains of a house. A gigantic tree branch had fallen on the house.

"This is Frank," Andy said, walking over to Grey and introducing the man. Frank offered his dirty hand, and Grey shook it.

"We're going to help Frank this afternoon," Andy said.

"Sounds good," Grey said. "You guys go on ahead. I'll wait for Trevor."

"Where is he?" Summer asked.

"He's . . . well, he needed to talk to Mira," said Grey.

Summer hopped down off the fallen tree trunk, her muddy boots splashing in a small puddle. She and Andy followed Frank into what was left of his front yard. Grey shoved his hands into the pockets of his shorts and waited for Trevor to return.

After about fifteen minutes, Grey became anxious. He started to walk back toward the checkpoint. *Maybe Trevor and Mira really hit it off,* he thought. But he doubted it. Even if the older girl *did* like Trevor, she was pretty much running the show here. She wouldn't just sit around and chat with a boy when there was so much work to be done.

The bus that Mary and the others had climbed onto at lunch was now gone. Only the short white bus that Grey and the other teens rode up in was left.

He saw Mira and Finn standing beside the bus. They were speaking with a volunteer, who offered Mira a bottle of water. Mira shook her head.

Trevor was nowhere to be found.

Grey looked around. *Where did he go?* There was a line of Port-o-Johns along the side of the road, farther down the road from the site, but it didn't look like he was there. Maybe Grey had just missed him entirely, and Trevor had taken a different route back to meet up with Summer and Andy.

Confused, Grey approached Mira. "Excuse me?" he said.

Mira turned to face him. Her eyes were piercing, but she also looked near exhaustion. Still, she was beautiful. "Can I help you?"

"Y-yeah," Grey stammered. "I'm uh . . . looking for my friend. His name is Trevor."

"Trevor? Is he a volunteer?" she asked.

"Yeah. Last I saw him, he was coming to talk to you," Grey explained.

Recognition dawned on Mira's face. "Oh!" she said. "Yes, Trevor. I spoke with him briefly and then saw him walk toward the bus. I assume he rode back with the other volunteers."

"What?" Grey blurted out. *That makes zero sense,* he thought. *There's no way Trevor would have up and left without telling me.*

"If you'd like, I can contact the staff at the community center and have them confirm that he's onboard when the bus arrives there," she said.

Grey nodded. "Yeah," he said, "That'd be good."

There was static on Mira's walkie-talkie. She unclipped it from her belt and said, "Excuse me," to Grey. Then she walked toward Finn, pressing the button on the side of the walkie-talkie and saying, "This is Mira."

Grey was baffled. Trevor, as unpredictable as he sometimes could be, would never just leave. Not when he knew Grey was waiting for him. Something wasn't right.

Wait. I'll just give him a call, Grey thought.

Grey dug a hand into his shorts pocket and grabbed his phone. He began to punch in Trevor's number when he saw the *NO SIGNAL* icon at the top of the screen.

"Of course," he muttered.

He held the phone up over his head and began to walk in circles, as if that could possibly help him get cell-phone service.

No luck.

Grey surveyed the wreckage. A sick, sinking feeling gnawed at his insides. Despite the blazing heat, he felt cold. Goose bumps covered his arms and made the hair on the back of his neck stand up.

Something is wrong, he thought. *Something has happened to Trevor.*

CHAPTER 7

Grey clutched the phone in his hand so tightly he thought it might shatter. His knuckles were white, and his whole body seemed to be shaking.

Trevor is out there, he thought as his eyes darted from one volunteer to another, hoping to spot his friend.

He held the phone up again, and he even went so far as to punch Trevor's number in and try to connect. Still, the phone had no signal.

Grey walked quickly along the road, dodging a pile of heavy boulders that were strewn about like children's toys that had been tossed aside and forgotten.

He cupped one hand around his mouth and called out, "Trevor?!"

A couple of people near him turned, but neither of them was Trevor.

Grey walked faster. His repeated shouts were not answered, except by their own echoes.

He could feel his heart racing. He imagined all sorts of terrible things that could have happened to his friend. Though the site was supposed to be safe enough for people to return to, it was still dangerous.

Don't panic yet, Grey told himself. *Maybe he's with Summer and Andy.*

Frank's house was on Grey's left, the enormous fallen tree trunk blocking its driveway. Grey made his way around it. As he did, he narrowly missed a giant crevice where the wet earth had cracked and split in two. The gash must have been at least six feet deep.

"Whoa!" he cried out, leaping over the cracked earth. He didn't remember seeing that earlier, when Frank had led Summer and Andy toward his home. *Is it some kind of sinkhole?* he thought. He made a mental note to tell Finn and Mira about it, in case it was something dangerous.

From the backyard, Grey heard the loud hum of a chainsaw as it ripped into wood.

He walked around the side of the wrecked home. Summer and Andy were in the sloping backyard. Frank held the chainsaw. He was removing smaller branches from the large chunk of tree that had landed on his property.

There was no sign of Trevor.

As Grey approached, Frank removed his clear safety goggles. Summer, who was kneeling in the dirt and cleaning what

appeared to be a vase, stood up when she saw him.

"Have either of you seen Trevor?" Grey asked, out of breath, as he looked from Summer to Andy.

Summer shook her head. "I thought you were waiting for him," she said.

"I was," Grey explained. "I even talked to Mira. She was almost certain that Trevor had left on the bus with Mary and the others."

"Maybe he really did leave," Andy said.

"No way," Grey said. "He wouldn't do that."

"Okay," Summer said. She placed the vase in the plastic bag at her feet and wiped her hands on her jeans. "Frank, we have to go look for our friend. We'll be back in a bit."

"Sure thing," Frank said as he fired up the chainsaw to begin his work again.

WOODSON

Andy, Summer, and Grey walked back out to the street to begin searching the area. They called out for Trevor. They asked every homeowner and volunteer who was still out working in the harsh heat if they'd seen him, but no one had.

"I'm going to head back and check in with Mira," Grey said after they'd walked up and down the block a couple of times. He could see her far in the distance, back at the checkpoint.

Summer pointed to a stretch of homes on their right — one-story ramblers with basements. A few were damaged but still standing. The roof of one had been split from the house's framework and sat half off the home, like a jar with an open lid. "We'll check behind there," Summer said.

But Grey didn't think Trevor would have been able to make it back there through all the debris. And why would he have gone there in the first place?

Grey began to walk back toward the checkpoint. He was halfway down the block when he heard Andy shouting, "Grey! Grey, come back!"

Grey turned. The lanky teen was in the street, waving his long arms over his head like he was stuck on an island and signaling to a passing rescue boat.

Despite the heat and the exhaustion he felt, Grey ran back to Andy and Summer.

"We can hear Trevor!" Andy said. "He's stuck in the basement over there." He pointed to where Summer stood next to the broken house, dwarfed by the piles of debris on either side of her.

"He is?" Grey was certain they were messing with him. *How could he be trapped in that basement?* he wondered. *It looks like it is impossible to even get near that house.*

His heart rate began to skyrocket as he and Andy walked around the side of the house, carefully making their way through the wreckage. When they got around back, Grey noticed that a wave of mud had crashed against the side of the home. Summer stood a little bit ahead of them, near one of the basement's wide windows. The windowpane had been shattered, leaving jagged edges like teeth around the frame.

When he got close to the window, Grey crouched down, placed his hands in the mud, and tried hard to peer into the basement. It was pitch black; if Trevor was down there, he couldn't see him.

"Trev!?" Grey called. Strangely, his voice did not echo. Instead, it was as if the basement swallowed the sound whole.

From the black, an arm suddenly shot out of the window. Its fingers clawed at the earth.

With it came a voice. "Grey! Grey, is that you?"

"Trevor!" Grey reached out and clasped his friend's hand. Trevor felt cold; in fact, the air coming from the basement was colder than Grey had expected.

In the shade of the house and the deep shadows of the basement, it was hard for Grey to see his friend. He saw the shape of Trevor's head and shoulders, and very faintly, his features. His eyes were wide.

"I didn't think anyone was going to hear me," Trevor said, relieved.

"How did you get down there, man?" Grey asked.

"I . . . I don't know," Trevor answered. "I was looking for you guys, and . . . and . . . what is that?! Do you feel that?"

Trevor released Grey's hand and vanished back into the darkness.

"Trev!" Grey yelled.

The ground began to rumble and shake, just like it had earlier when they were at

Mary's house. Grey staggered back, away from the window. Pebbles and stones rained down from the house's roof, tumbling from the pile of mud pressing against the siding of the house. Summer grabbed one of Grey's arms, Andy the other, and they pulled him back from the house.

The quake ended abruptly, leaving nothing but silence in its wake.

"Hey, Trev! You okay in there, dude?" Grey yelled.

No answer.

"One of us should run back and get Mira and some adults," said Summer. "We need help."

Grey heard what Summer said, but he chose to ignore her. All he was concerned with was Trevor.

What if part of the house fell in on him? he thought. *What if he's hurt? Or worse?*

"Come on," Grey said. "Say something."

"I'm okay." Trevor's voice was weaker than before. But he was still there.

"Are you hurt?" Grey asked.

"No."

Summer stepped forward carefully. The dirt around the window was looser now. "Do you see anything in there?" she asked Trevor. "Like another way out?"

"It's really dark," he said. "The only light is from the window."

Summer lowered herself to one knee. "Reach out your hands again — both this time," she said. "We'll try to pull you up."

Before Trevor could respond, the dirt around Summer's feet gave way. It gushed like a waterfall down through the window, taking Summer with it. She fell onto her back, letting out a gasp. As the mud moved beneath her, Summer turned onto her stomach and tried to claw her way back to safety. But the avalanche was too strong. It was almost like the ground was pulling at her, grabbing her in its arms and drawing her down into the darkness.

That's . . . that's crazy, Grey thought as he stood there, stunned.

"Summer!" Andy dove forward, trying hard to pull her free. But soon, he, too, was caught up in the deluge of sand, rocks, dirt, and twigs.

Grey took a step toward them, then froze as the earth around his feet began to shift. He retreated, away from the house. He could only watch as both brother and sister were swallowed by the great gap of the broken window, disappearing along with Trevor into the blackness of the basement.

CHAPTER 8

Grey was rooted to the spot like a statue, too stunned by what had just happened to move. One minute, Summer and Andy were on level ground with him, and the next, they were gone. He watched as the stream of sliding dirt, mud, and debris slowed, then stopped.

"Guys?" he called out. He dared not step any closer to the window. "Summer? Andy? Are you all right?!"

There was coughing, then Summer's voice, meek and uncertain. She said something that Grey couldn't hear.

Then Andy called out, "Grey! Are you still out there?"

Grey let out the breath he was holding. "Yeah," he answered. "I'm here, but I'm going to get help."

"Hurry," Andy said. "Summer's legs are buried in the dirt, and I can't get her free."

"Oh, man," Grey whispered. Then, louder, "What about Trevor?"

"He's here," said Andy. "He's okay, just . . . he's just standing there. I think he's in shock or something."

"Okay, I'll be right back," Grey said.

"Hurry!" Andy pleaded.

Grey backed away from the house, nearly tripping on a twisted tree root. He stumbled, recovered his balance, and then ran as fast as he could toward the street.

The sun beat down on the back of his neck. He could feel the sweat pouring off him. His heart thundered in his chest. "Help!" he cried out, his voice carrying over the ruined site. He waved his arms wildly over his head. "Somebody help! My friends are trapped!"

A few of the homeowners and volunteers turned at the noise. In the distance, Grey saw Finn step into the road and turn toward him.

When he was about fifty yards from the checkpoint, Grey stopped running. He had a really painful cramp in his side, so he bent over, placed his hands on his knees, and tried hard to catch his breath.

Finn jogged down to meet him. "What's the emergency?" he asked.

"My friends . . ." Grey sucked in deep breaths of hot, thick air. "They're stuck."

"Show me."

Grey led Finn back along the street, toward the house where Trevor, Summer, and Andy were trapped. As they went, others joined them — including Mira — until almost all of the remaining volunteers and homeowners were following them. Some whispered questions to one another, but many were tired and silent.

When they reached the house, Finn turned to the others and said, "Stay here, in case the ground is unstable." Then he nodded at Grey. "Lead the way."

Grey, Finn, and Mira walked around the side of the house. Grey held his breath again. He was afraid that they would find the ground had collapsed again, that even more dirt, sand, and debris had fallen in through the broken window, that his friends would be permanently trapped in the basement.

Thankfully, everything looked the same.

"Hello?" Finn called out in his deep, booming voice. He crouched down and pulled a flashlight from his pocket. "Is there anyone down there?"

"Yeah," Andy said. He sounded weaker than he had when Grey had left just minutes before.

"How many of you are trapped?" Finn asked.

Andy's face appeared in the window, lit by the glow of Finn's flashlight. He squinted. Grey noticed the thick layer of dirt coating Andy's face now. It made his wide, bloodshot eyes look brighter than usual. "Three of us," Andy said. "One's stuck under a mound of dirt. The other is in shock."

Finn nodded, then turned to Mira. "Radio down to base," he said. "An emergency vehicle can be here in no time. Go."

"Got it," Mira said.

Grey watched, helpless, as she brought the walkie-talkie to her mouth and said, "Site to base, site to base. Do you copy?"

There was a burst of static . . . then nothing.

"Site to base, do you copy?" Mira repeated. She scrunched up her eyebrows.

"What is it?" Grey asked. "Is something wrong?"

Mira banged the walkie-talkie with the side of her hand. The red light on top flickered, then faded out. "The battery . . . it's dead." She tried it again and got the same response.

"What about Finn's? Or an extra battery?" Grey asked. He could feel the anxiety coursing through his veins. He was terrified for his friends.

"Finn and I are sharing one," Mira said. "There are more batteries, though, in the front seat of the bus. They should be charged and ready to go."

"Great." Grey snatched the walkie-talkie from her. "I'll be back as soon as I can."

A low, distant rumble echoed across the sky. Grey looked up. He hadn't been paying attention, hadn't noticed the line of clouds blotting out the sun or the darker clouds coming in from the ocean.

It's going to rain, he thought. *Again.*

And that meant they needed to get away from the site quickly.

There was no time to lose.

With that, he took off again down the street, back toward the checkpoint.

Grey's lungs were burning. He hadn't sprinted this much in ages — not since he and Trevor had played on a basketball team together in seventh grade, before they'd decided to quit the team and start skateboarding instead.

Trevor, Grey thought. *I can't let him down.*

Thinking of his friend brought renewed adrenaline to Grey. It made him push his tired legs to run even faster. His Angels ball cap went fluttering off his head. He felt it slip away and briefly swiped at it before it tumbled through the air, but then he hurried along without it.

He made it to the bus just as another distant thunderclap echoed through the sky. The bus driver was nowhere to be found. "Hello?" Grey called, pounding on the bus's closed door. "Hello!"

Grey reached his fingers into the slot between the bus door and the body of the vehicle. He grunted, strained, and pulled, until the door opened just far enough for him to slide inside. Once on the bus, Grey used the control to open the door the rest of the way.

"Batteries, batteries," he muttered, searching the front seats. He found a couple of hard plastic cases. One was marked FIRST AID. The other was black and unmarked. It rested on the bus floor under the seat.

Grey slid the case out. He popped the latches on the side and opened it wide.

"Bingo!"

Two walkie-talkies lay nestled in thick foam inside the case. There were also a couple of spare batteries and a charging station with a plug-in.

Grey grabbed one of the spare batteries out of the case. He removed the dead battery from the back of the walkie-talkie, then replaced it with the fresh one.

Then he clicked on the walkie-talkie. The red light glowed bright. "Oh, thank you, thank you," Grey whispered.

But then suddenly it faded out.

"No!" He swatted at the walkie-talkie, pressing all the buttons. "Hello?" he called into it. "Hello? *Anyone?!*"

The new battery must also *be dead,* Grey thought.

"You've got to be *kidding* me!" Grey took the battery, wound up, and chucked it down the length of the bus. It struck the floor and clanged against the metal legs of the bus seats.

He tried the other battery and got the same results. Everything appeared to be dead.

We're trapped. It's almost as if someone doesn't want us communicating with the base down below, Grey thought. He shook his head and tried to clear his thoughts.

He stepped off the bus, not sure what to do next. There was no cell signal, and there were no walkie-talkie batteries. He could run . . . try to make it down the hill to the edge of the disaster zone before it rained. It was only a mile or two.

It'd be just like running around the track at school, he told himself. *Probably even easier, since most of it is downhill.*

That's what I'll do, Grey decided. *I'll make a break for it and hope that I can outrun the weather.*

Grey stretched his legs, took a deep breath . . . and stopped. His eyes had drifted across the street, to the house Summer had pointed out earlier, the one left standing by the storm. It looked the same as before except there was no figure standing in the window, like Summer had sworn she'd seen earlier.

There was, however, a light.

Grey hadn't noticed it in the brilliantly sunny sky, but now that clouds had covered up the sun, he could tell that a light was on in a second-story room. Which meant someone *did* still live in that house. And that they had light.

And if they had light, they had to have a generator. And that meant they had to have . . . power.

"If I can plug in the battery charger just long enough to get it to work," Grey said, thinking aloud, "then I can get help faster than if I run."

A bolt of lightning streaked across the dark sky, startling him. The storm was close; it would be upon them in no time.

Grey climbed back aboard the bus, gathered the case containing the battery charger, dropped his walkie-talkie and one of the spare batteries in, and snapped it closed.

Then he took off across the street, climbing the small hill to the only house left untouched by Mother Nature's wrath.

CHAPTER 9

Four wooden stairs led to the front porch. As Grey approached, a cold stone of uncertainty grew in the pit of his stomach, and he felt like the house was a living thing, watching his every move. Up close, he could see the house had indeed suffered some damage. The siding was covered in mud, which had caused the paint to flake and peel. Shingles were missing from the roof. The cement foundation was cracked in a few places.

Grey climbed the porch steps and was surprised when they didn't creak under his weight. The porch ran the length of the house, long planks of wood stained with dirt and grime. There was no chair or swing, as Grey often expected to see on porches like this one. There was also no screen door, just a heavy wooden one with a small window that was so high up, Grey would need to be on tiptoe to see through it.

He hesitated before knocking, his fist mere inches from the door. *What are you doing?* he asked himself. *This is no time to be afraid. Your friends' lives are at stake.*

As if it were waiting for the perfect moment to strike, the sky released the loudest clap of thunder yet. Its earth-shattering rumble startled Grey so much that he dropped the plastic case containing the walkie-talkie charger.

Grey picked up the case and knocked on the door, anxious beyond belief. He waited for the door to swing wide.

But no one answered.

He tried knocking again, this time louder.

Still, no one came to the door.

Grey walked across the porch, toward a window so covered in grit that he couldn't see inside. He used his palm to smear away some of the dirt, then cupped his hands around his eyes to peer in.

The room looked empty. Just wooden floors and painted walls.

He went back to the door and knocked even harder.

"Hello!" he yelled as loud as he could. "Is anyone home?"

On the last pounding knock, the door opened just a crack, inviting him inside. But no one stood behind the door, so Grey wasn't sure how it had opened.

Earlier, the light was coming from upstairs somewhere, Grey thought. *Maybe the person who lives here is hard of hearing or something like that.*

Grey scooped the black case off the porch and shoved the door open wide.

He stepped into the empty room, and immediately, his body tensed up. In his mind, he felt like he was walking into the belly of a breathing beast. Grey could almost sense the walls of the home expanding and contracting like lungs.

"Hello?" Grey's voice echoed through the empty living room and dining room. Through the doorway of the dining room, he could just barely see the kitchen tucked away toward the rear of the house. There was a set of wooden stairs leading up to the second level. And everything was coated in a thin layer of dust and grime.

Grey went to the foot of the stairs and then craned his neck to look up. He didn't see anything and couldn't hear any movement.

Maybe the lights are on, but nobody's home, he thought.

Not wanting to waste time, Grey searched the living room for a place to plug in the charger. If the someone who lived here came back while he was there, Grey was sure he or she would understand the situation.

But after scanning the living room, he couldn't find any power outlets. Even in old homes, there were usually at least a few in each room, low on the wall, near the molding. But this strange house didn't seem to have a single one.

Tiny pinpricks of rain began to hit the windows as the edge of the storm reached Winston Hills. The sound of the wind, rain, and thunder was enough to send Grey into a panic.

A door in the kitchen swung open suddenly, slamming against the wall and shuddering on its hinges. In the living room, Grey jumped back, frightened. Then, a low, crackling sound drifted up from the basement, and the floor began to shake.

"Is someone here?" Grey asked. The pitch of his voice had gone up to nearly a squeak. "Listen, my friends are in trouble. Please, if someone is here and your house has power, I *need* to call down to our base camp. *Please.*"

A lump had formed in Grey's throat, and he realized he was on the verge of crying.

"Come closer." The voice came from the basement. "I'm . . . down here . . ."

Every nerve in Grey's body told him to run, but somehow, for some reason, he walked through the living room and into the kitchen, where the door to the basement was open wide, like the unhinged jaw of a creature.

Grey stumbled forward, reaching the doorway. A set of splintered wooden stairs led down into the basement. It was dark, and the smell of rotten leaves and decay crawling out was so thick it made Grey's stomach turn. A single lightbulb dangled on a chain.

And there, standing in the dim glow of the bulb, was a teenage boy.

A boy Grey knew very well.

"Trevor?"

CHAPTER 10

"Grey!" Trevor shouted from the bottom of the broken stairs. "Oh man, I was hoping you'd find me."

As Grey's eyes grew accustomed to the darkness of the basement, he saw that his friend's legs were buried up to the shin in mud and muck, like the earth had clawed its way up and held fast to him.

"But — but you're . . ." Grey couldn't wrap his mind around what he saw. He'd just spoken with Trevor, trapped in the basement of a house an entire block away. He'd run here to call for help. Finding

Trevor in *this* house, in *this* basement? It just didn't make sense.

"You have to help me," Trevor said, reaching out his arm. "Get me out of here."

"What's going on?" Grey asked. "How are you *here*?"

"I was talking to Mira, and then . . . I saw something. Here at the house. So I came up to check it out and . . . it trapped me."

"What trapped you?"

"The house. The mud. There's something in the *mud*," Trevor said. "It's taking us over, one by one — sucking us down into the ground and creating clones out of the earth. I saw it . . . it *made* a version of me."

That's not possible, Grey told himself.

Grey didn't believe in any of that supernatural garbage. Aliens? Lame. Bigfoot? A guy in a suit. Ghosts? People seeing what they wanted to see. So his brain struggled to understand how there were two Trevors. He didn't believe what his friend was telling him.

Not until the house began to move on its own.

The stucco wall beside Grey shuddered and expanded. It pressed in toward him, like a bulging, bubbling mass. Grey stumbled backward, tripped over his feet, and fell to the floor. He brought one arm up to protect his eyes in case the bubble popped.

It didn't. The bulging mass on the wall changed shape, and he could see that it was clay and mud.

The house is made of mud.

Grey looked down at his hands, which were pressed against the kitchen's tile floor. He curled his fingers, scratching at the dirty tiles as dirt caked under his nails.

We have to get out of here.

He staggered to his feet. Outside, a clap of thunder shook the house. The rain was coming down harder now. Grey heard it slam against the roof and the walls. He pictured the mud house crumbling to wet chunks of earth, burying Trevor and him underneath it.

"There is no escape," a woman's voice said. Grey looked up. The mass on the wall had formed into the shape of a human face, and it was staring back at him.

He was looking right at Mary.

It didn't look entirely like the real Mary, the one Grey had first met, the one who cried about losing her photo albums. The face in the wall was not completely formed. It was unlined, too smooth to be human. And the eyes looked tired, hollow.

All of them, he thought, remembering Mary and the man at the community center and every other soul he'd seen looking tired and empty and lost. *They've all been replaced by whatever is lurking in the ground.*

Mary's face smoothed and disappeared, the mud molding itself into another face. This time, Grey was looking at Summer. It changed again, and he saw Andy. It changed once more, and he was looking at himself.

"Grey? Are you still there?!" Trevor called.

Hearing his friend's voice snapped Grey back from the shock that was threatening to envelope him. "Yeah," he said. "I'm here." He staggered forward, his eyes never leaving the wall and its horrifying mirror image of himself. He reached the open doorway and crouched down.

"Can you reach up?" he asked, stretching his arm toward Trevor as far as he possibly could. Trevor leaned forward, trying unsuccessfully to pull himself out of the mud. Their hands were mere inches apart.

"I can't . . . reach you," Grey said. "I can't do it."

"You can," Trevor said. "I know you can."

Grey lay flat on his stomach, momentarily forgetting that the floor on which he now lay was part of whatever living, moving creature trapped Trevor. He reached his arm out.

"We're not . . . gonna make it out of here," Grey said.

Trevor's hand snaked up and clamped down on Grey's wrist. "Yes, we are," Trevor said. "Everything is just fine."

Everything is just fine.

The words turned Grey's blood cold. He'd heard them before. From the man at the community center. From Mary.

No. Not Trevor, too.

Grey pulled his arm back toward him. Caught by surprise, Trevor lost his grip. "Dude, what are you doing?" he asked.

Grey shook his head. "You're not Trevor, are you?"

"Of course I am. Come on. I'm your best friend, Greyson."

"You're trying to trick me," said Grey. "This is all one big game, isn't it?"

He stood, stumbled back a step.

Down in the basement, Trevor smiled. It was a wicked grin. The lines on his face disappeared, and the mud at his feet receded back into the ground. "Join us, Greyson," it said, its voice cold and calculating and not at all Trevor's anymore.

"No." Grey's voice was barely a whisper.

"I'm sorry to hear that," not-Trevor said.

Grey ran.

He headed toward the front door of the house. Around him, the walls began to vibrate, to expand. Chunks of earth fell from the ceiling, landing all around him. He covered his head with his arms just as a rocky piece of debris struck him. It glanced off his arm, sending shivers of pain from his fingers to his shoulder. The walkie-talkie and the black plastic case were long forgotten. There was no need to help Summer and Andy and Trevor. Grey knew that the mud had already taken them.

He dashed through the living room, heading toward the front door. Beneath his feet, the floor trembled. It cracked open, creating a giant crevice under him. Thinking quickly, he leaped to one side, narrowly avoiding the gap.

In front of him, fresh mud oozed in to block the door. The house was closing in on itself, doing its best to trap Grey inside. If he didn't hurry, the door would disappear entirely. Grey lowered his shoulder and barreled into it.

The door crumbled as he crashed through it. He fell hard onto the porch, the wind knocked out of his lungs. He lay on his back, watching as the hole he'd created in the door disappeared.

Suddenly, a muddy hand appeared, stretching out of the porch floor. It grabbed Grey's shoulder and pulled at his shirt.

"Ahhh!" Grey screamed as he jumped up, breaking the clay hand's grip. He leaped off the porch, back down to the soaked ground.

Behind him, the entire house collapsed in an earth-shattering roar. It fell to pieces, chunks of soaked clay and mud, until it was nothing but a pulsing pile of earth.

The smoky charcoal clouds in the sky had opened, and the rain was coming down hard. Grey looked out at the ruin, at the wrecked homes and fallen trees and layers of mud covering all of it.

I have to warn the others, he thought, *get them out of here before it's too late.*

Grey took off running down the street, back to Mira, Finn, and whoever else was left in Winston Hills.

CHAPTER 11

Grey's shoes slapped hard against the muddy street. Large puddles were already pooling on the cement, and streams of water carved down the curbs toward drainpipes that were already clogged. It was like crossing a minefield, and Grey tried his hardest to avoid the largest puddles and sinkholes.

His clothes were drenched, and his shirt clung to his chest and weighed heavily on his shoulders. He wanted to peel it off and cast it aside. But he didn't have time to stop and struggle with it.

Grey could see a couple of volunteers farther down the street. Their orange vests blazed bright against the murky landscape. Water ran from his soaked hair down into his eyes. He smeared it away with one dirty hand and looked down just in time to see his Angels baseball cap floating in the middle of a puddle.

All around him, the mud was beginning to move and split open. Human forms with no features were crawling out of the muck, raising themselves up and staggering to their feet like newborn animals.

"Mira!" Grey shouted. "Finn! Get out of there! Your lives are in danger!"

The volunteers up ahead began to advance on Grey. He didn't have to see their hollow eyes to know that they'd already turned inhuman.

Grey went toward the back of the house, where he'd left Mira and the others. His feet sloshed in the muck, the very substance that was trying to capture him. Hands emerged from the mud, dripping wet, with fingers made of tree roots and twigs. Grey kicked one away and leaped over another.

In the backyard, he saw the remaining volunteers and homeowners — those who hadn't yet been taken by the mud — fending off those who had. He recognized a couple of teenagers from his group and watched them struggle with the others.

"Over here!" Mira waved her arms wildly at him. Grey saw her near the window, which was now completely clogged with mud and water. It bubbled and gurgled. A giant tree root was wrapped around her shin.

Grey ran over to her. He grabbed the tree root with both hands and pulled with all of his remaining strength. It peeled away from Mira's leg, freeing her.

"Come on!" she shouted.

"Where's Finn?" Grey asked.

She pointed at the gurgling basement.

"We need to get out of here!" Grey shouted to the few remaining survivors.

"How?!" Mira asked.

"The bus!"

He grabbed her hand, and they set off across the yard together toward the street. Along the way, Mira pulled another teenager to safety, while Grey shoved a tree branch into the chest of another mud creature and rescued the volunteer it was attacking. A few others saw them dashing for safety and joined them.

In total, eight more volunteers and residents joined Grey and Mira in their retreat.

They splashed and sloshed through the rain and the mud, panicked questions slipping from their mouths: "What are they?" and "What's happening?" and "Is this *real*?"

They didn't know what Grey knew. They didn't know how many others the earth had already swallowed.

Grey cast a brief glance behind them. Sure enough, like a mass of stumbling zombies, the mud creatures were chasing after them. Still more were forming out of the muck to join in.

"Hurry!" he yelled, hoping to spur on the survivors.

As they neared the checkpoint, Grey searched through the pouring rain for the bus. For the briefest of seconds, he expected the bus to be gone, expected that it had been made of mud like the collapsed house and was now nothing more than a pile of oozing muck.

It was there, though.

And the door was still wide open, just as Grey had left it when he'd been there earlier searching for the walkie-talkie batteries.

He pointed. "There!" he shouted to the rest.

Grey was the first to reach the bus. He leaped onto the steps and scrambled aboard, out of the downpour. Even though his heart was racing from panic and shock, he still had sense enough to scan the bus and make sure none of the mud creatures were hidden inside.

It was clean.

Mira climbed aboard by herself, but others needed help. One boy had twisted his ankle and hobbled over to the bus. Frank was next to him, and he helped lift the boy onto the stairs while Grey grabbed the boy's arms and pulled him to safety.

Behind him, Mira was fumbling around near the driver's seat.

"Are the keys in the ignition?" he asked.

"Yeah!"

It's a miracle, he thought.

Frank was the last of the survivors to make it onto the bus. The wall of mud people chasing after him was close.

Grey wrapped both hands around the metal handle that controlled the door and forcefully shoved it back. The door closed with a bang.

"Get us out of here quick!" he yelled. Mira fell into the driver's seat. She twisted the key in the ignition, and the bus roared to life.

We're going to make it!

A wet slap on the bus door made Grey jump and turn. A face was pressed against the glass. Trevor's face.

"Let me in, Grey!" he shouted. "Come on, dude! Hurry! They're coming!"

Grey shook his head slowly. *It's not him*, he had to remind himself. *It's not Trevor.*

"Isn't that your friend?" Mira asked, terrified.

"No," Grey said. "Just . . . go!"

Mira threw the bus into gear. Rain pelted the windshield, making it impossible to see. She searched around, found the windshield wiper switch, and clicked it on. The wipers whooshed furiously back and forth.

The vehicle lurched forward, then stopped suddenly.

"They're holding on to us!" Frank shouted. He and the others were huddled together in the middle of the bus. Some had their arms wrapped around each other. Frank was peering out one of the rain- and mud-streaked windows.

Mira stomped on the gas pedal, but the bus didn't budge. Grey heard the whir of spinning tires. The mud creature that was impersonating Trevor was still at the door. He smiled evilly.

The mud creatures began to pound on the bus, smacking, sloshing strikes. The ground beneath the bus began to shake.

"The road . . ." A crying woman in the back pointed out the emergency door. "The road is . . . cracking open. And it's . . . getting closer."

If the bus didn't move soon, it would fall into the crack.

Grey peered out the windshield at the road in front of them. As he did, the left side of the road split and fell, creating an enormous sinkhole. Rain, streaming downhill already, poured into the opening, creating a deep pool of brown water and mud.

"Come on, come on," Grey muttered as Mira pressed the gas pedal to the floor.

Over her shoulder, the window suddenly shattered. She screamed as rain and wind streamed in through the opening. A hand, dripping wet, reached in. It clawed at her shoulder and then at her hair.

"Mira!" Grey leaped forward to rescue her. He grabbed her right arm in both of his and pulled her toward him with all his might.

Grey fell back against the bus door, banging his head and falling to his rear on the floor of the bus. It was as if Mira had suddenly let go, letting Grey fall backward . . . except he was still holding her arm. Stunned, he looked down at his hands.

In his grip was Mira's right arm. It had torn away from her body at the shoulder.

"No," Grey whispered. For a long, horrified moment, he thought Mira had been seriously injured. And then he saw that the arm was not made of flesh and blood and bone.

It was made of mud.

He looked up from his spot on the floor, near the steps. Mira still sat in the driver's seat, missing arm and all. As he watched, mud emerged from her shoulder and back. It started as a gnarled stump, then twisted and molded itself into a new arm, all the way down to the tips of her fingers.

Mira smiled at him and wiggled the fingers of her new hand. "Don't worry, Grey," she said. "Everything is just fine."

Hastily, Grey threw the clump of dirt that used to be Mira's arm aside. It landed with a dull thud on the bus floor.

He pulled himself up, slowly getting to his feet as he looked around for any signs of danger. The assault on the outside of the bus had ceased.

They've won, Grey thought. *There's too many of them, and there's no way to escape. They're done playing their silly little game with us.*

Grey looked down at the other volunteers and homeowners on the bus, huddled together in the aisle. On their faces were looks of fright and confusion.

He opened his mouth to explain, to say something to comfort them.

The bus began to move.

Grey stumbled back, clutching at the front seat in order to stay upright. The bus took off down the hill, bouncing and rattling. But Grey couldn't take his eyes off the road. The wipers were still working feverishly to clear the windshield, making it hard to see. But Grey knew that Mira was not driving them to safety.

She's driving right toward the sinkhole.

Ahead of them, the hole in the road bubbled and roiled. Grey clutched the seat with both hands until his fingers were bone white. He thought of his mother, safe — for now — at the community center. She was probably watching a weather report, wondering if her son had made it out of the mudslide zone before the rain set in. He thought of Trevor, his best friend since they were in kindergarten, and remembered splashing through rain puddles together in brightly colored galoshes and rain slickers, laughing as they each tried to drench the other. He thought of Summer, Andy, Mira, Mary, Frank, Finn, and all the rest of the people he'd met that day. He thought of the other mudslides around the country and wondered how many of the horrible mud creatures had already taken over the lives of normal, everyday people.

When the bus was feet away from the sinkhole, the wide windshield filled with nothing but mud now, Grey squeezed his eyes shut.

The bus struck the sinkhole and was swallowed up.

CHAPTER 12

"Welcome to Action Ten Nightly News. I'm Robert Carlson," the newscaster announced, his eyes looking tired. "Our top story tonight continues to be the devastated Hollisworth neighborhood of Winston Hills, where Mother Nature's wrath strikes once more. Still reeling from the mudslide that damaged nearly everything in its wake, relief crews and volunteers faced another freak rainstorm this afternoon. Natalie Gates continues to report live outside the Hollisworth Community Center, with more on the story. Natalie?"

"Thank you, Robert," the reporter said, standing in a sunny parking lot. "Like the five-day storm that caused the mudslide, the storm today also appeared as if from nowhere. When all was said and done, it dropped over three inches of water in an hour, leaving the already flooded neighborhood of Winston Hills nothing more than mud and rivers of dirty water. Residents and volunteers, who were just cleared yesterday to return to the area, were once more forced to flee as the ground became unstable. The final busload was not able to get out before the storm began. The vehicle fell into a sinkhole in the road, but thankfully, no one was on board at the time.

"I have with me one of the survivors of the freak storm, and son of Dana Bennell, the Hollisworth Director of Community Services, fifteen-year-old Greyson Bennell. Greyson, what was it like in Winston Hills during the rainstorm?"

"It was scary," the teenage boy said, his face grim. "But we all waited at the checkpoint with our team leaders, Finn and Mira. My friend Trevor was with me the whole time. We knew that help was on its way."

"And did you see the bus fall into the sinkhole?" Natalie asked.

"Yes. One minute it was there, the next it was just gone."

"Well, Action Ten News is glad to see that everyone is accounted for, and that everyone is doing well."

"Thanks," said Greyson. "Everything is just fine."

"'Everything is just fine.' Hopeful words from a brave teenager. With Action Ten News, I'm Natalie Gates. Back to you, Robert."

GLOSSARY

adrenaline (uh-DREN-uh-lin) — a chemical produced by your body when you sense danger

baffled (BAF-uld) — confused

casualties (KAZH-uhl-teez) — people injured or killed in an accident, war, or natural disaster

checkpoint (CHEK-point) — a point at which a check is performed

condensation (kahn-den-SAY-shuhn) — the changing of a gas or vapor into its liquid form

crevice (KREV-iss) — a narrow opening in something

deduction (di-DUHK-shuhn) — something that is figured out from a little information

deluge (DEL-yooj) — an overwhelming amount of something, usually water

dramatically (druh-MAT-ik-lee) — when something is done in an over-the-top way

generator (JEN-uh-ray-tur) — a machine that produces electricity

homeowner (HOME-ohn-ur) — someone who owns a home

meteorologists (mee-tee-uh-RAH-luh-jists) — experts in the study of the earth's atmosphere

minefield (MINE-feeld) — something that has many dangers or risks; an area set with mines

silhouette (sil-uh-WET) — a dark outline of someone or something

sinkhole (SINGK-hole) — a hollow place in which water collects

DISCUSSION QUESTIONS

1. In this story, was it easy to tell who was a mud clone and who was a real person? Discuss why or why not.

2. Why is it important that Summer spotted the silhouette in the second-floor window of the undamaged house in Winston Hills? Talk about the significance of that sighting.

3. Grey had to shut the bus door in Trevor's (or clone-Trevor's) face when the mud creatures were chasing him and the other volunteers. Discuss how you would have felt if you'd been in his position.

WRITING PROMPTS

1. At the end of the book, which characters do you think are real people and which do you think are mud creatures? Write a list of the characters and your reasons for thinking whether or not each is a real person.

2. Imagine you are a newspaper reporter in Hollisworth. Write an article on the aftermath of the mudslide, including interviews with residents.

3. Natural disasters happen often. In addition to mudslides, they include floods, tornadoes, hurricanes, monsoons, blizzards, droughts, and earthquakes. Research a natural disaster that has occurred recently, and write a report explaining what happened.

ABOUT THE AUTHOR

Brandon Terrell has been a lifelong fan of all things spooky, scary, and downright creepy. He is also the author of numerous children's books, including six volumes in the Tony Hawk's 900 Revolution series, several Sports Illustrated Kids graphic novels, and a You Choose chapter book featuring Batman. When not hunched over his laptop writing, Brandon enjoys watching movies (horror movies especially!), reading, baseball, and spending time with his wife and two children in Minnesota.

ABOUT THE ILLUSTRATOR

Nelson Evergreen lives on the south coast of the United Kingdom with his partner and their imaginary cat. Evergreen is a comic artist, illustrator, and general all-around doodler of whatever nonsense pops into his head. He contributes regularly to the British underground comics scene, and he is currently writing and illustrating a number of graphic novel and picture book hybrids for older children.

DANGEROUS DOUBLES

While it is unlikely that we will ever come face to face with our own mud clones, we can't seem to stop ourselves from coming up with stories about doubles or imposters.

European folklore tells of human children being snatched from their cradles and secretly replaced by trolls, fairies, or elves. These imposters are called changelings, and only the child's odd behavior ever caused the parent to suspect that a switch had occurred. One of the more gruesome ways to confirm a child wasn't human was to expose him or her to harm. Many tales speak of a suspicious mother getting ready to throw the child into a fire. Before hitting the flames, the changeling reverted to its true form and fled. Sometimes the human child was returned, and sometimes he or she remained lost, never to be seen again.